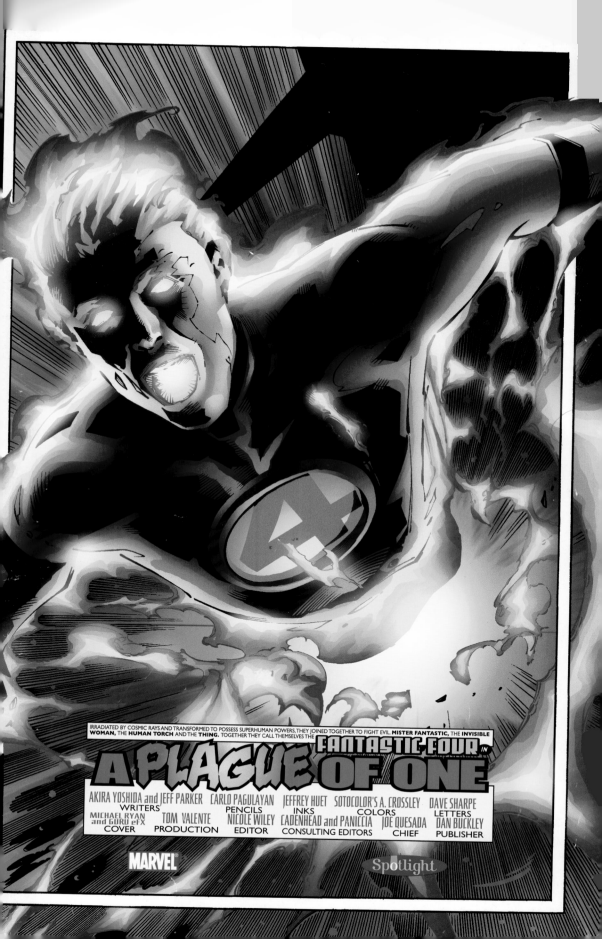

IRRADIATED BY COSMIC RAYS AND TRANSFORMED TO POSSESS SUPERHUMAN POWERS, THEY JOINED TOGETHER TO FIGHT EVIL. **MISTER FANTASTIC,** THE **INVISIBLE WOMAN,** THE **HUMAN TORCH** AND THE **THING.** TOGETHER THEY CALL THEMSELVES THE **FANTASTIC FOUR** IN

A PLAGUE OF ONE

AKIRA YOSHIDA and JEFF PARKER
WRITERS

CARLO PAGULAYAN
PENCILS

JEFFREY HUET
INKS

SOTOCOLOR'S A. CROSSLEY
COLORS

DAVE SHARPE
LETTERS

MICHAEL RYAN
and GURU eFX
COVER

TOM VALENTE
PRODUCTION

NICOLE WILEY
EDITOR

CADENHEAD and PANICCIA
CONSULTING EDITORS

JOE QUESADA
CHIEF

DAN BUCKLEY
PUBLISHER

VISIT US AT
www.abdopublishing.com

Spotlight library bound edition © 2007. Spotlight is a division of ABDO Publishing Company, Edina, Minnesota.

Cataloging Data

Yoshida, Akira
 Fantastic Four in a plague of one / Akira Yoshida and Jeff Parker, writers ; Carlo Pagulayan, pencils ; Jeffrey Huet, inks. -- Library bound ed.
  p. cm. -- (Fantastic Four)
 Summary: Irradiated by cosmic rays and transformed to possess superhuman powers, Mr. Fantastic, the Invisible Woman, the Human Torch, and the Thing join together to fight evil.
 "Marvel age"--Cover.
 Revision of the September 2005 issue of Marvel adventures Fantastic Four.
 ISBN-13: 978-1-59961-203-4
 ISBN-10: 1-59961-203-8
 1. Fantastic Four (Fictitious characters)--Comic books, strips, etc.--Fiction. 2. Graphic novels. I. Parker, Jeff. II. Title. III. Title: A plague of one IV. Series.

 741.5dc22

All Spotlight books are reinforced library binding
and manufactured in the United States of America

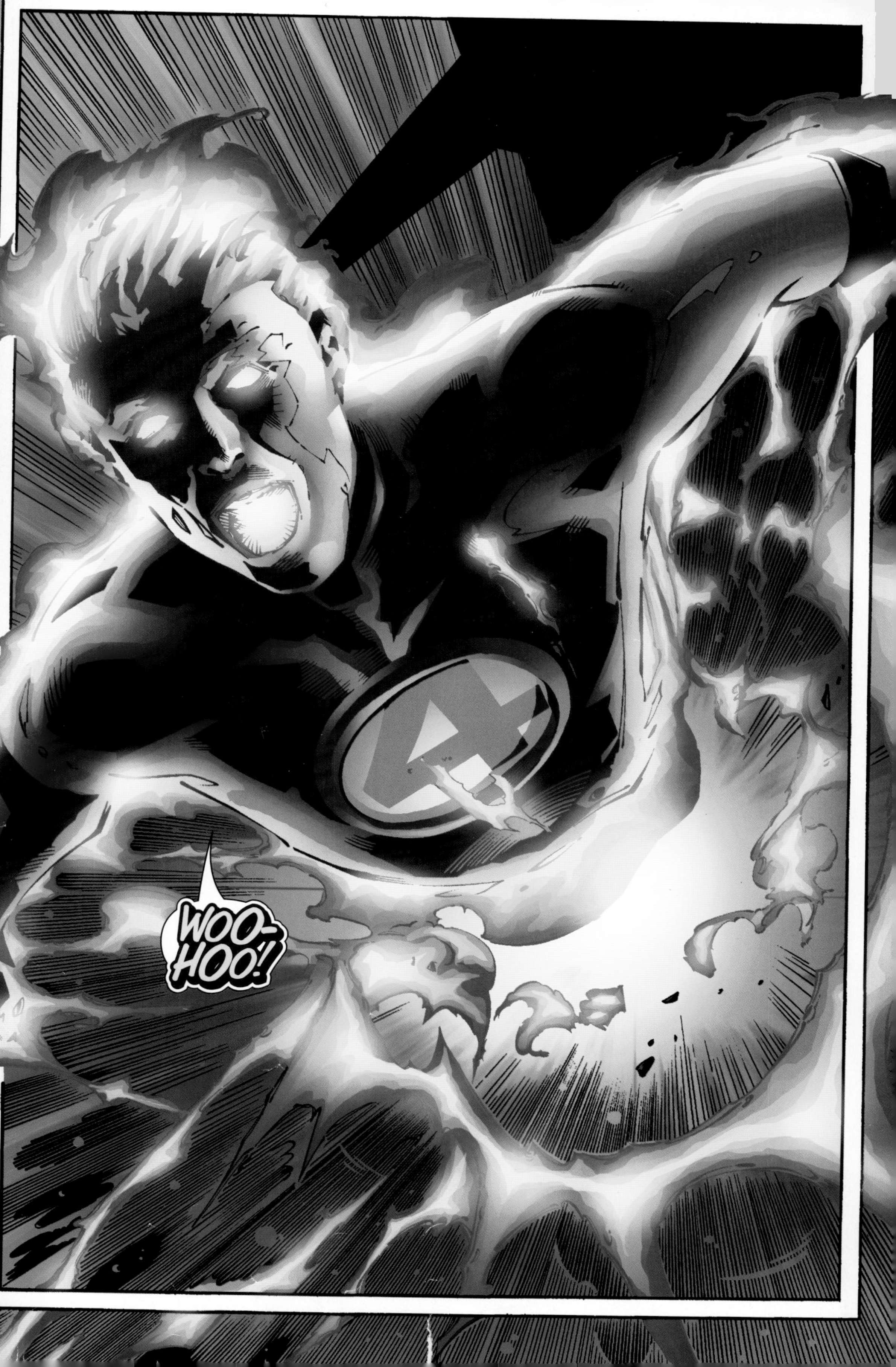
WOO-HOO!

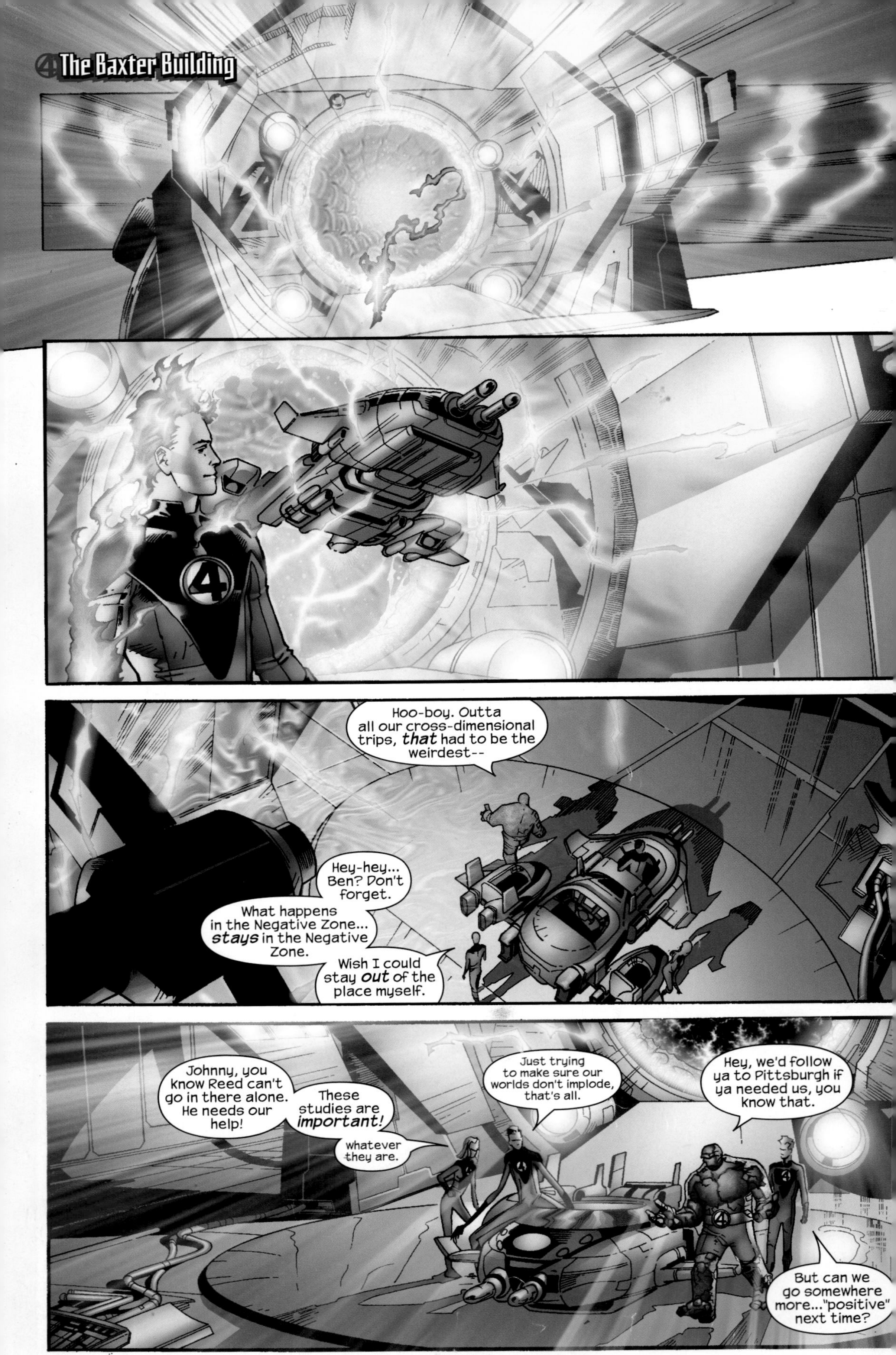
The Baxter Building
Hoo-boy. Outta all our cross-dimensional trips, *that* had to be the weirdest--
Hey-hey... Ben? Don't forget.
What happens in the Negative Zone... *stays* in the Negative Zone.
Wish I could stay *out* of the place myself.
Johnny, you know Reed can't go in there alone. He needs our help!
These studies are *important!*
whatever they are.
Just trying to make sure our worlds don't implode, that's all.
Hey, we'd follow ya to Pittsburgh if ya needed us, you know that.
But can we go somewhere more..."positive" next time?

Noted. I'll see if I can't find some analysis that needs to be done in Hawaii.

Now yer talkin'.

Around one of the big wave surf competitions, too!

~Whew!~ How can you even think straight, let alone joke, after a trip like that?

Who's joking?

So who wants hot wings?

Me! I do!

Sounds good, boys...

KLICK
BLEEP
PLIP

But I owe someone a date tonight.

You remembered!

Your loss, lovebirds.

HHHHHRRRRRRMMMMM

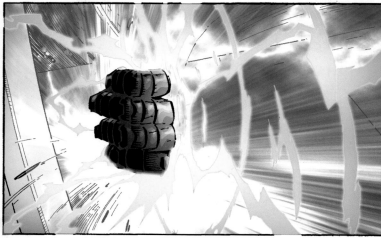

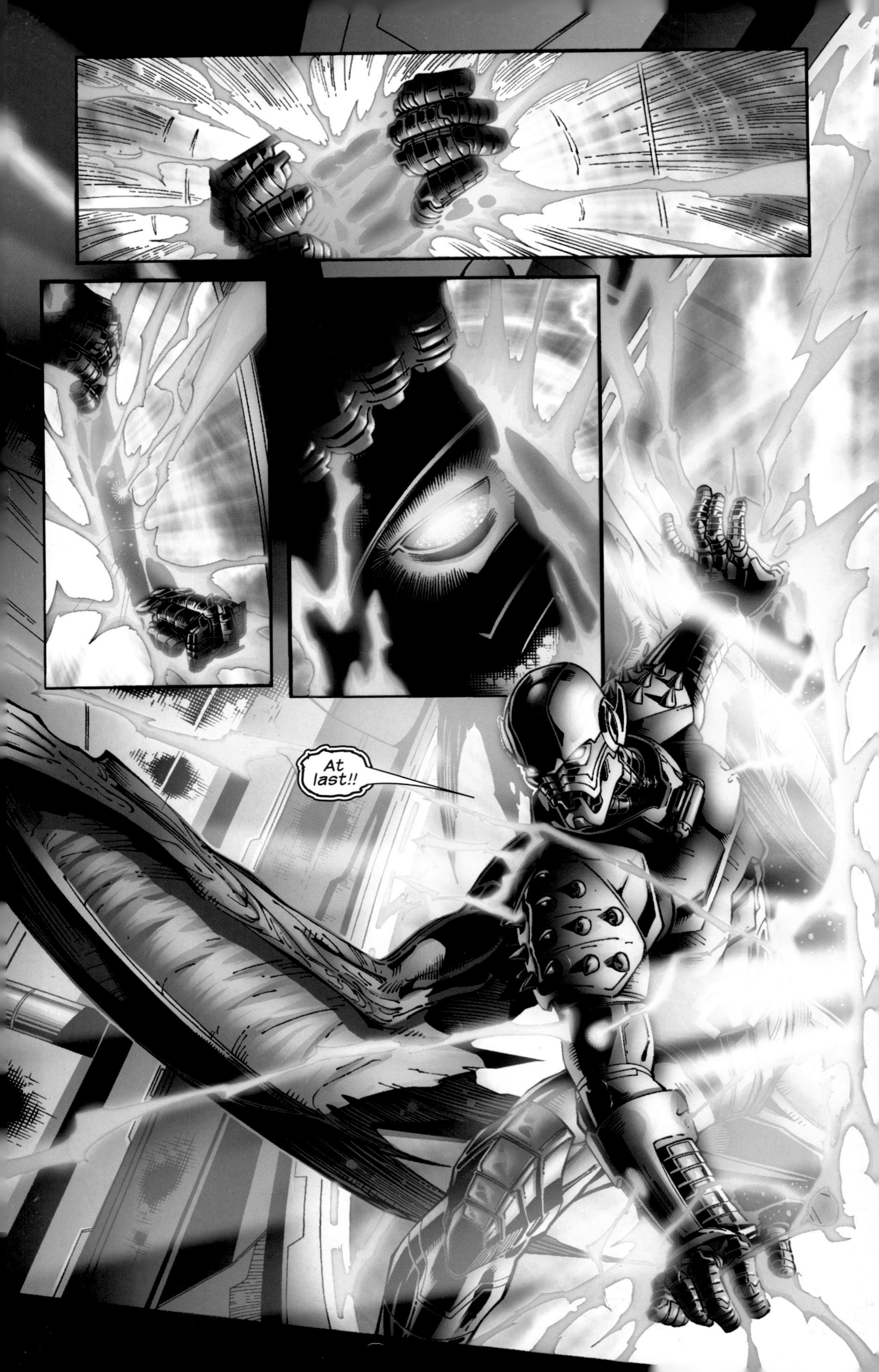
At last!!

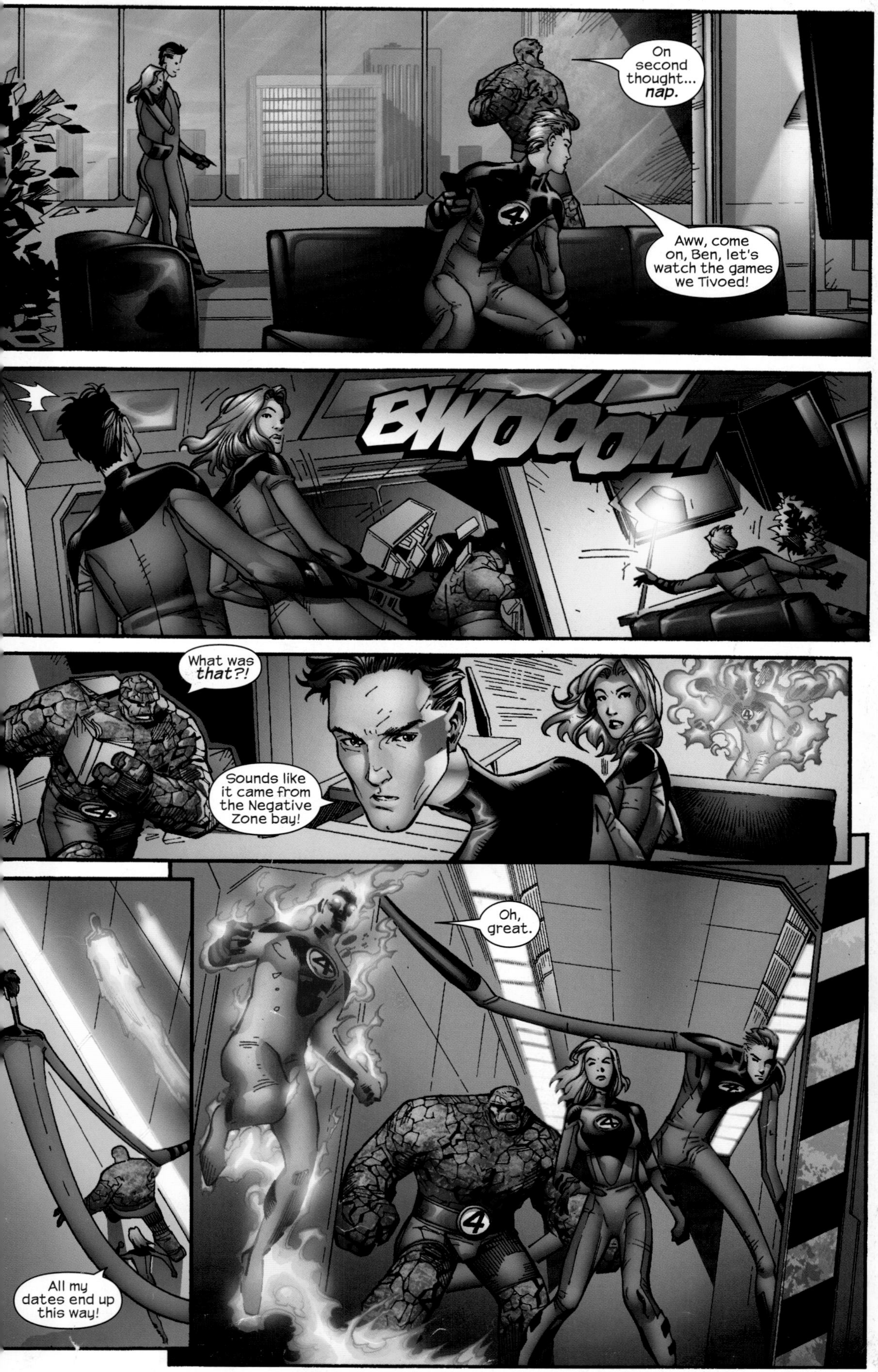
On second thought... *nap.*
Aww, come on, Ben, let's watch the games we Tivoed!
BWOOOM
What was *that?!*
Sounds like it came from the Negative Zone bay!
Oh, great.
All my dates end up this way!

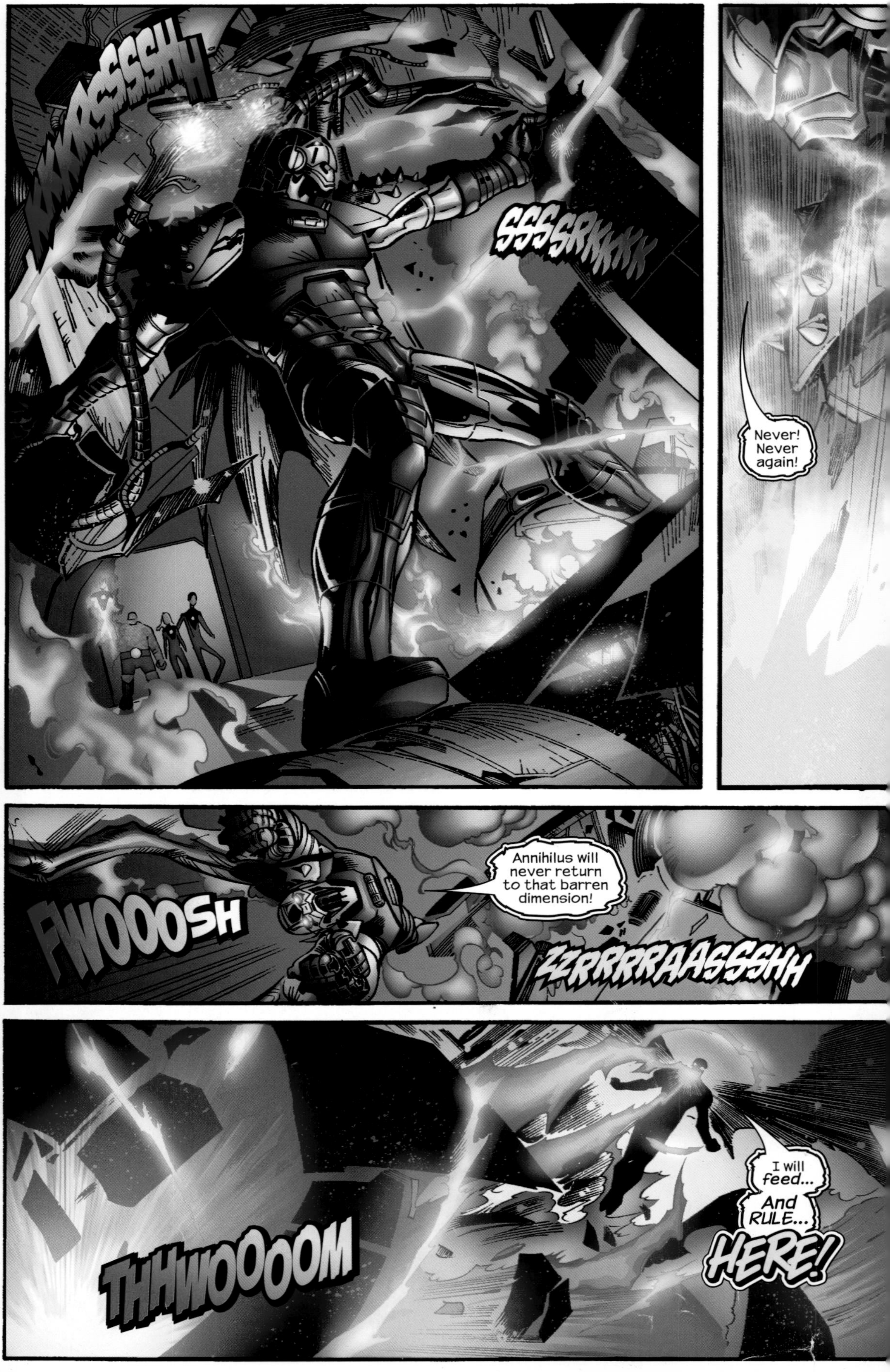
KKRASSSSHH
SSSSRKKKK
Never! Never again!
FWOOOSH
Annihilus will never return to that barren dimension!
ZZRRRRAASSSHH
THHWOOOOM
I will feed...
And RULE...
HERE!

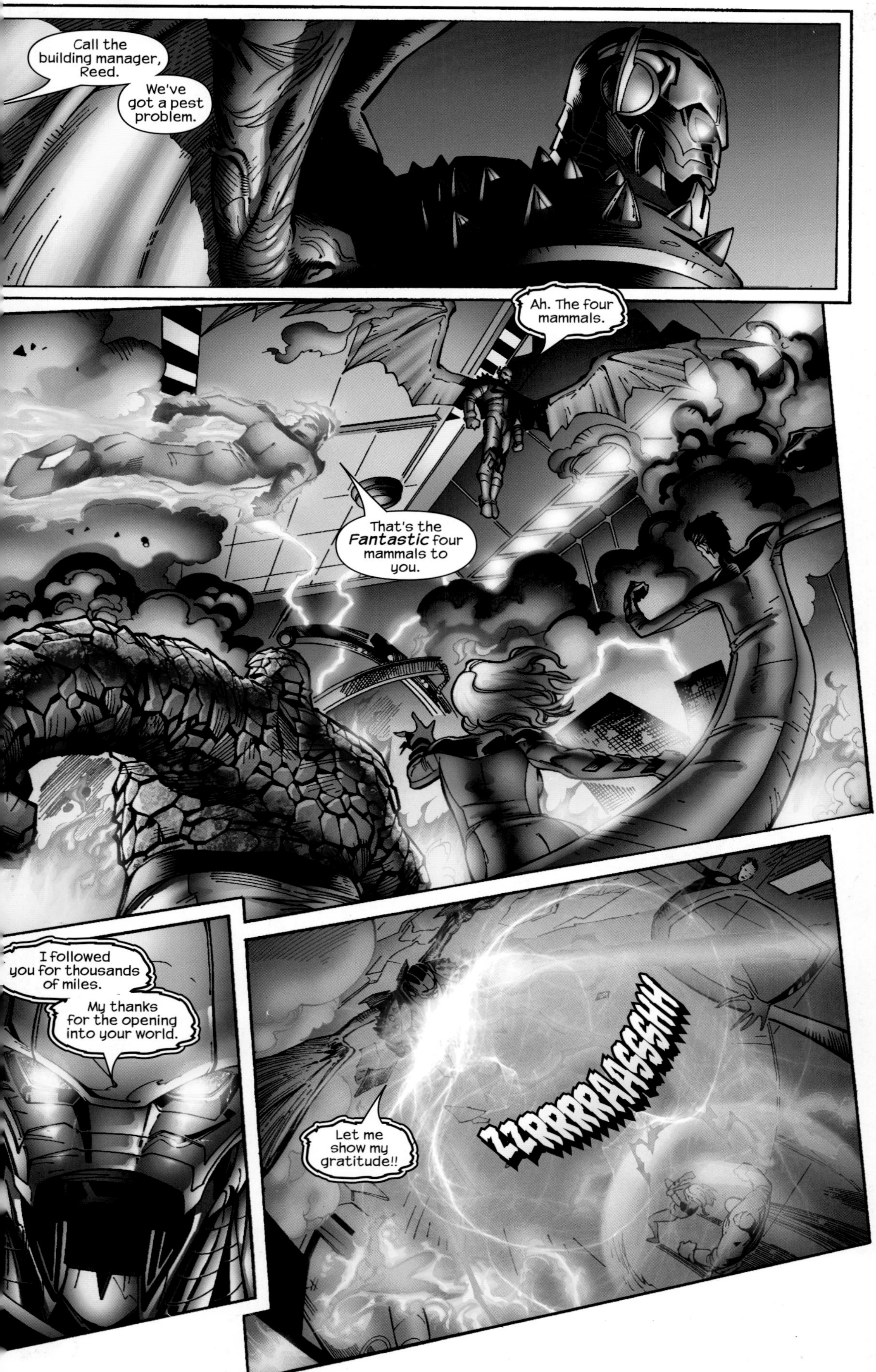
Call the building manager, Reed.
We've got a pest problem.
Ah. The four mammals.
That's the *Fantastic* four mammals to you.
I followed you for thousands of miles.
My thanks for the opening into your world.
Let me show my gratitude!!
ZZRRRRAASSHH

Bring it on, Annoy-us.

ANNIHILUS!

You just keep coming back...

...like a moth to a flame!

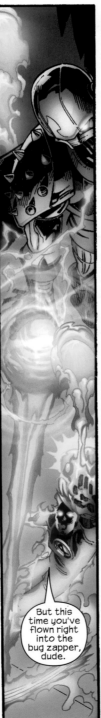

But this time you've flown right into the bug zapper, dude.

You command great power, boy...

...but you are still just flesh.

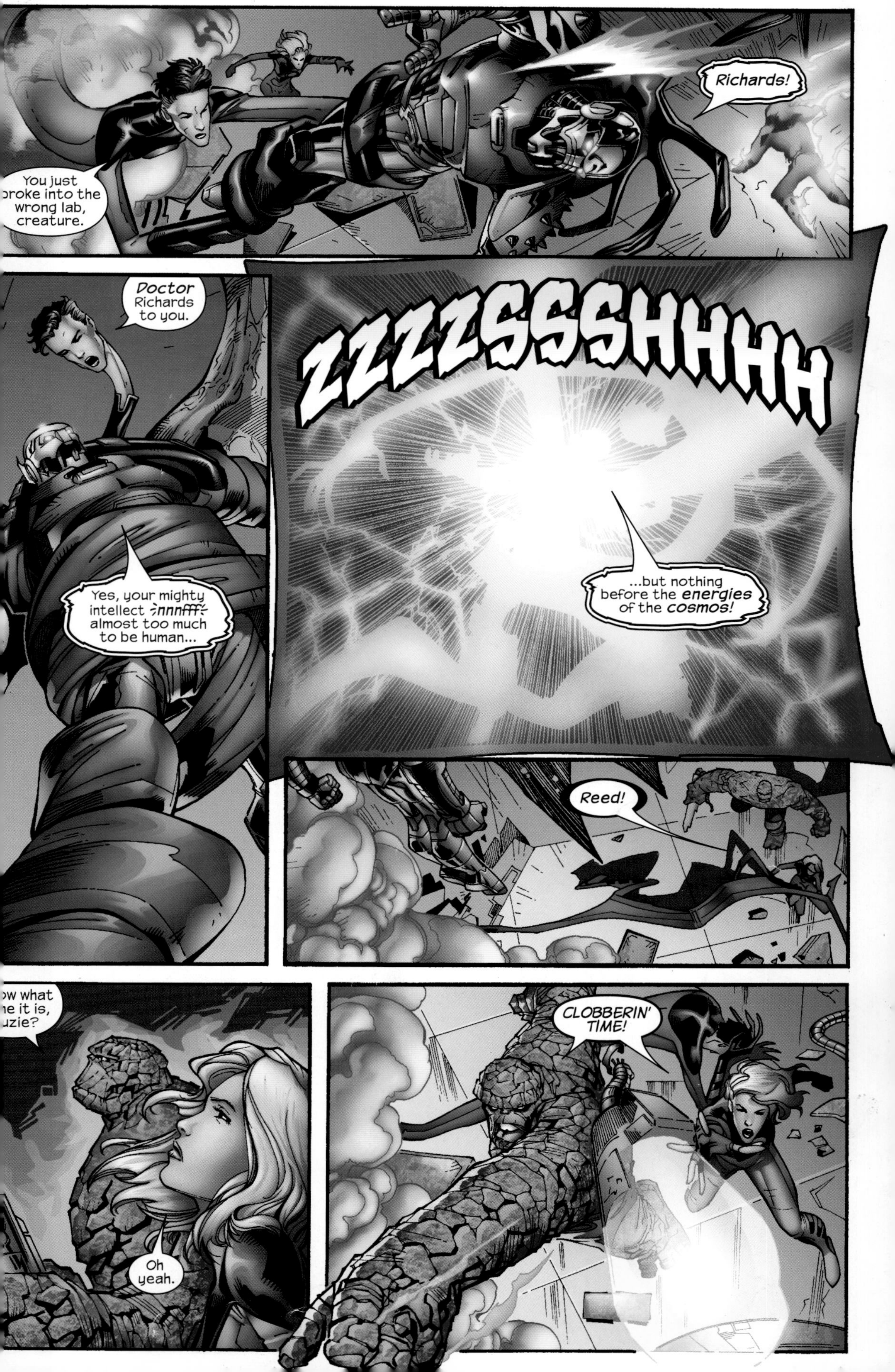
Richards!
You just broke into the wrong lab, creature.
Doctor Richards to you.
Yes, your mighty intellect -nnnfff- almost too much to be human...
ZZZZSSSHHHH
...but nothing before the energies of the cosmos!
Reed!
Oh yeah.
CLOBBERIN' TIME!

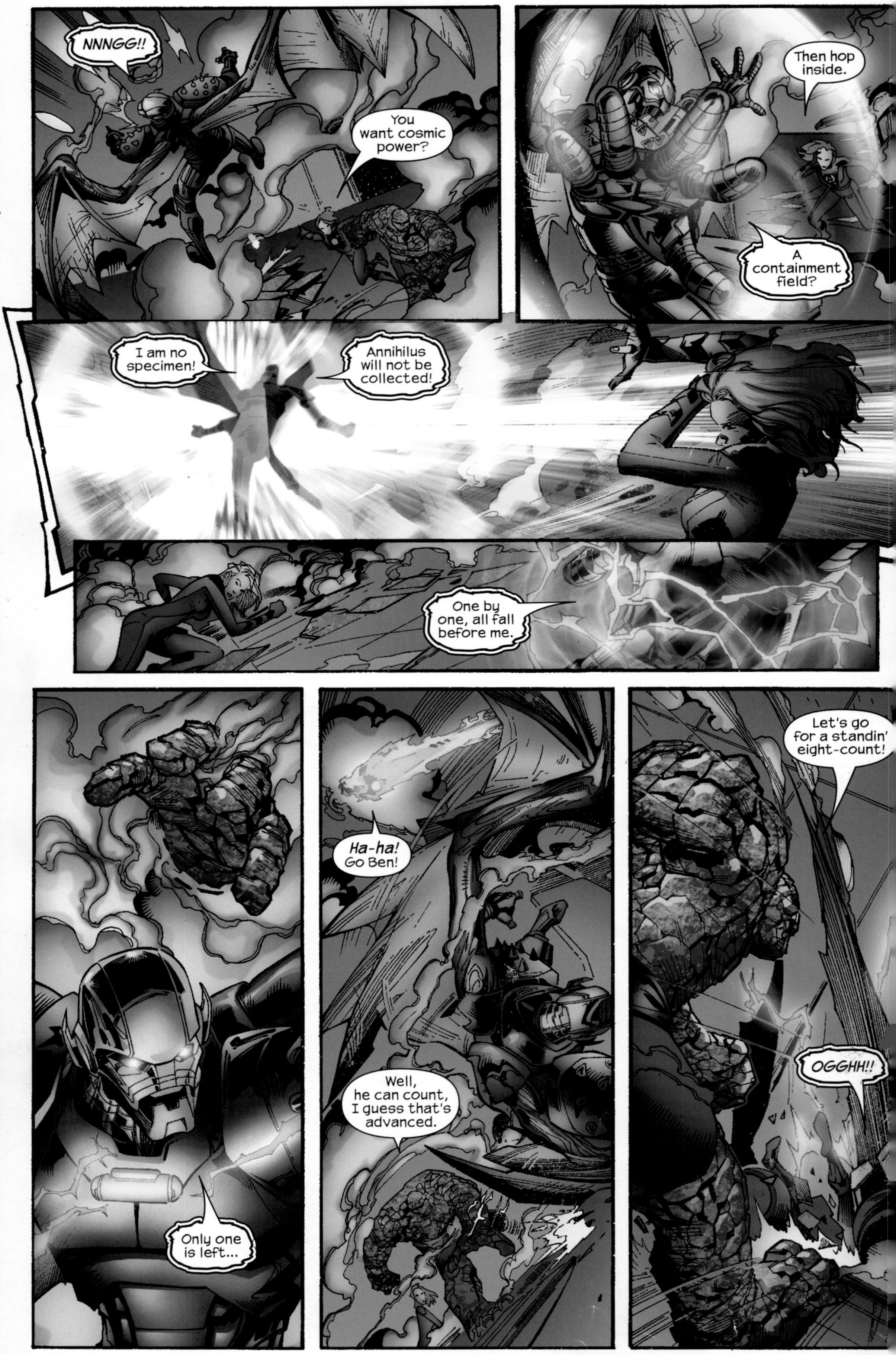
NNNGG!!
You want cosmic power?
Then hop inside.
A containment field?
I am no specimen!
Annihilus will not be collected!
One by one, all fall before me.
Only one is left...
Ha-ha! Go Ben!
Well, he can count, I guess that's advanced.
Let's go for a standin' eight-count!
OGGHH!!

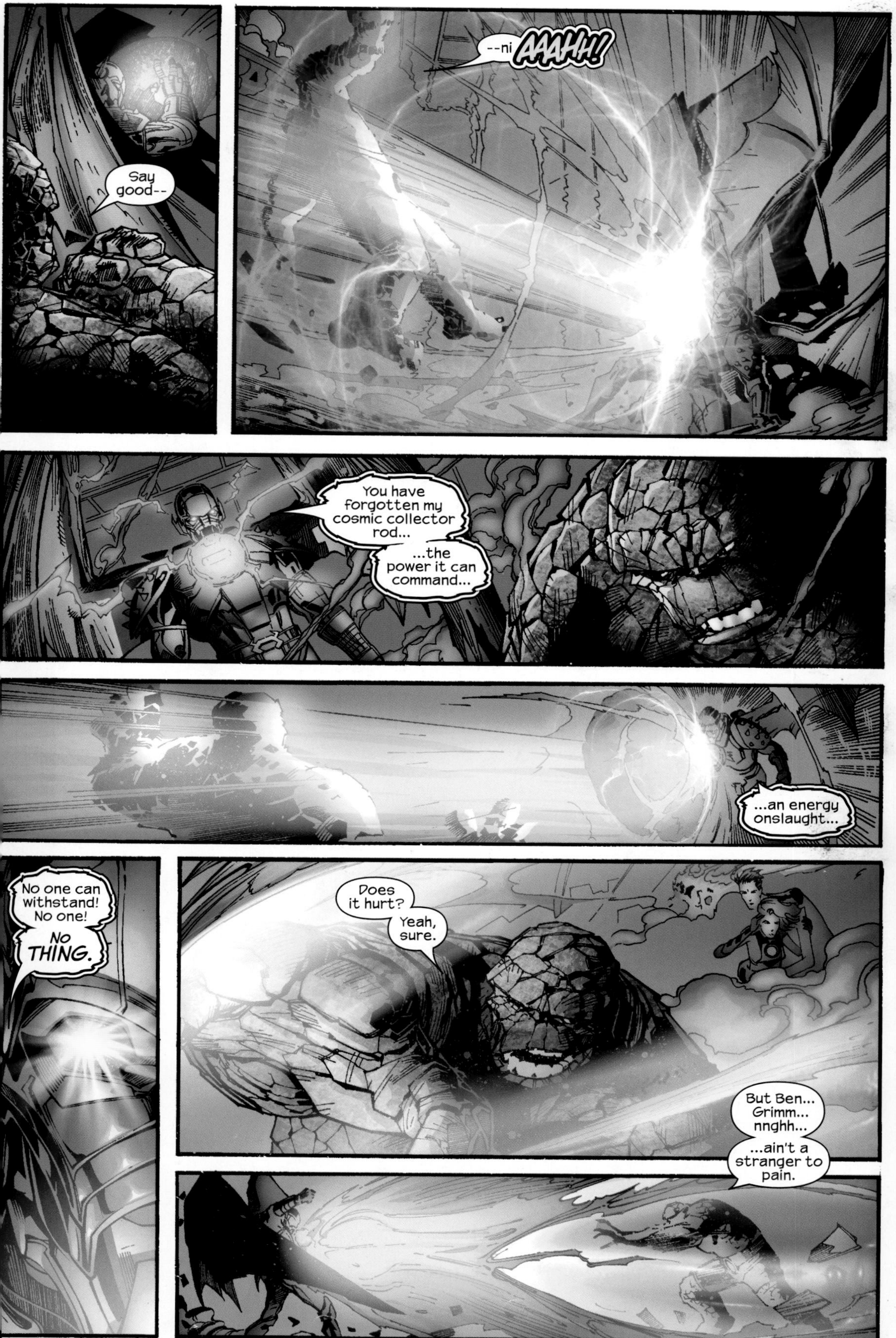
Say good--
--ni AAAHH!
You have forgotten my cosmic collector rod...
...the power it can command...
...an energy onslaught...
No one can withstand! No one!
NO THING.
Does it hurt?
Yeah, sure.
But Ben... Grimm... nnghh...
...ain't a stranger to pain.

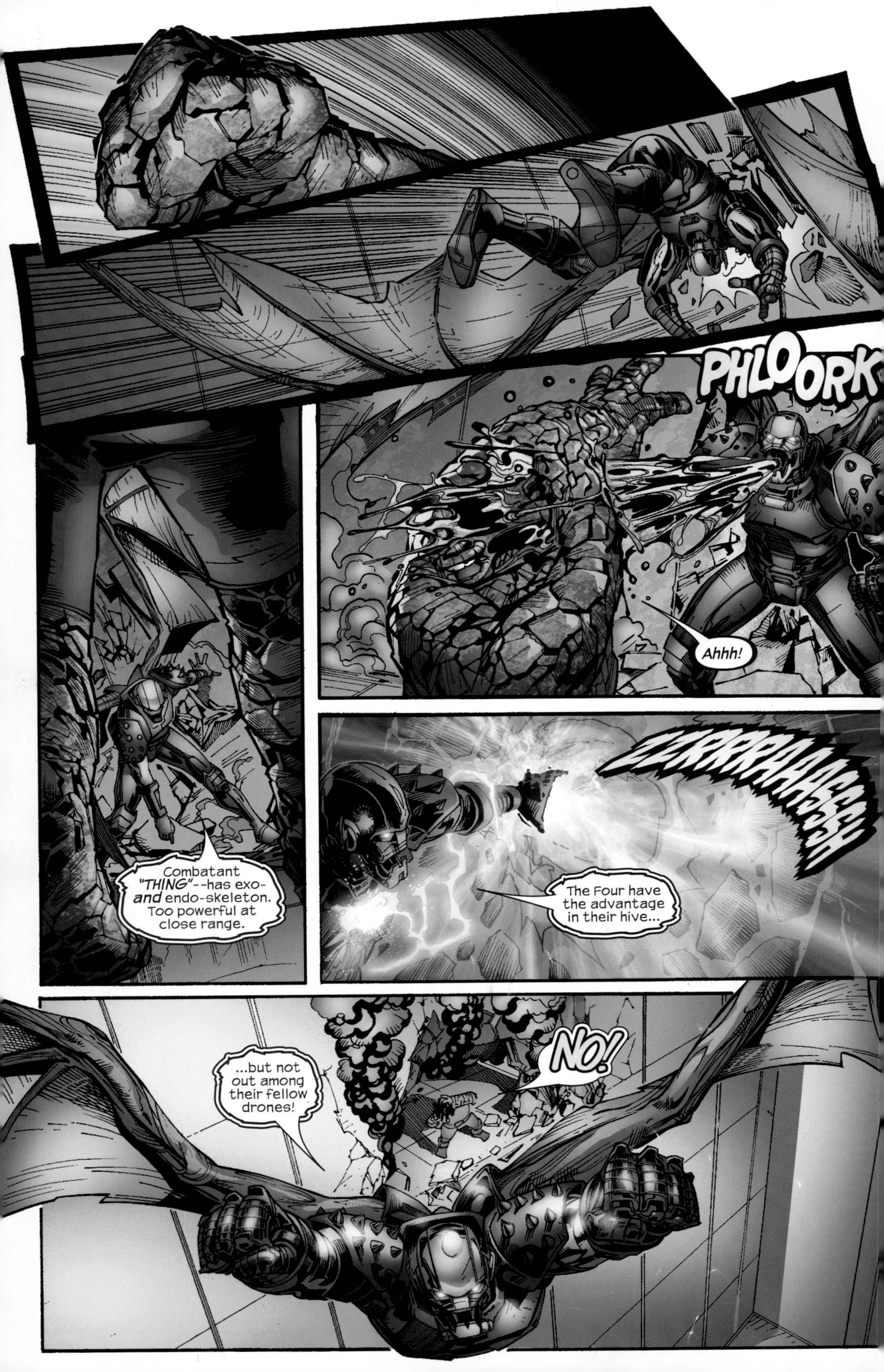
PHLOORK
Ahhh!
Combatant "THING"--has exo- and endo-skeleton. Too powerful at close range.
ZZRRRAAACCH
The Four have the advantage in their hive...
...but not out among their fellow drones!
NO!

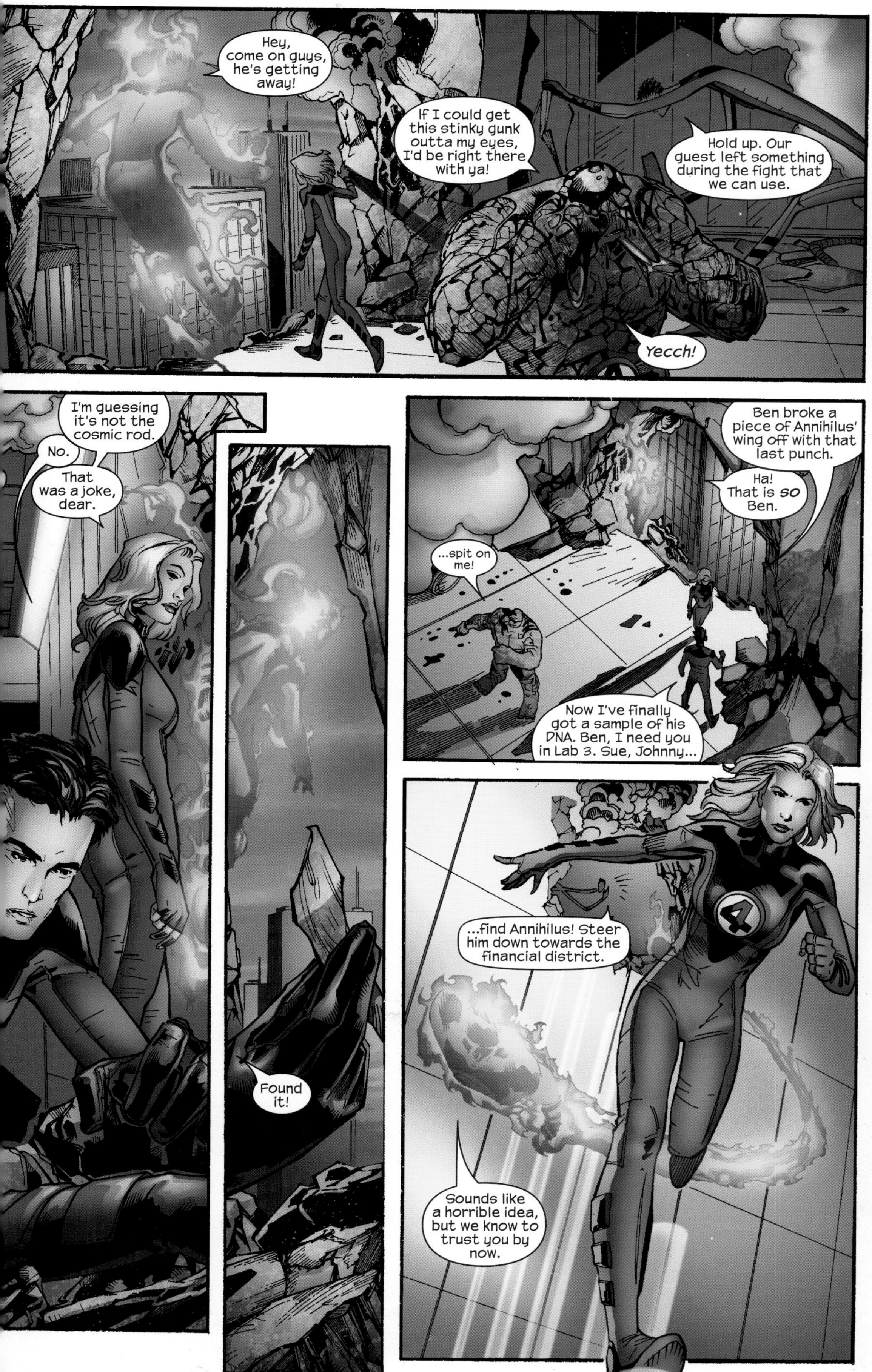

Hey, come on guys, he's getting away!
If I could get this stinky gunk outta my eyes, I'd be right there with ya!
Hold up. Our guest left something during the fight that we can use.
Yecch!
I'm guessing it's not the cosmic rod.
No.
That was a joke, dear.
Found it!
Ben broke a piece of Annihilus' wing off with that last punch.
Ha! That is *SO* Ben.
...spit on me!
Now I've finally got a sample of his DNA. Ben, I need you in Lab 3. Sue, Johnny...
...find Annihilus! Steer him down towards the financial district.
Sounds like a horrible idea, but we know to trust you by now.

Ahhhh. Now that gets the red out. Who knew that creep chewed tobacco?

That tar-like substance is a defense mechanism...

...similar to what our own grasshoppers spit when picked up.

Remember, Annihilus is an Insectoid being, just as we're mammals.

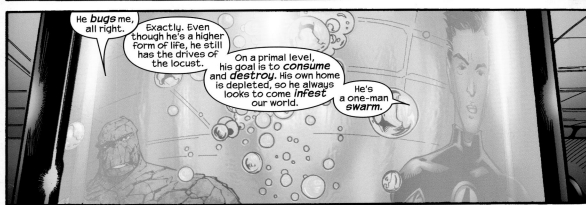

He *bugs* me, all right.

Exactly. Even though he's a higher form of life, he still has the drives of the locust.

On a primal level, his goal is to *consume* and *destroy*. His own home is depleted, so he always looks to come *infest* our world.

He's a one-man *swarm*.

Do you just like seein' me wear wacky gear? Izzat it?

I thought this up a while back but didn't have a DNA sample to key the solution to before.

This calls for heavy lifting, which is why I asked you to stay behind.

That, and to keep you and Annihilus from demolishing lower Manhattan.

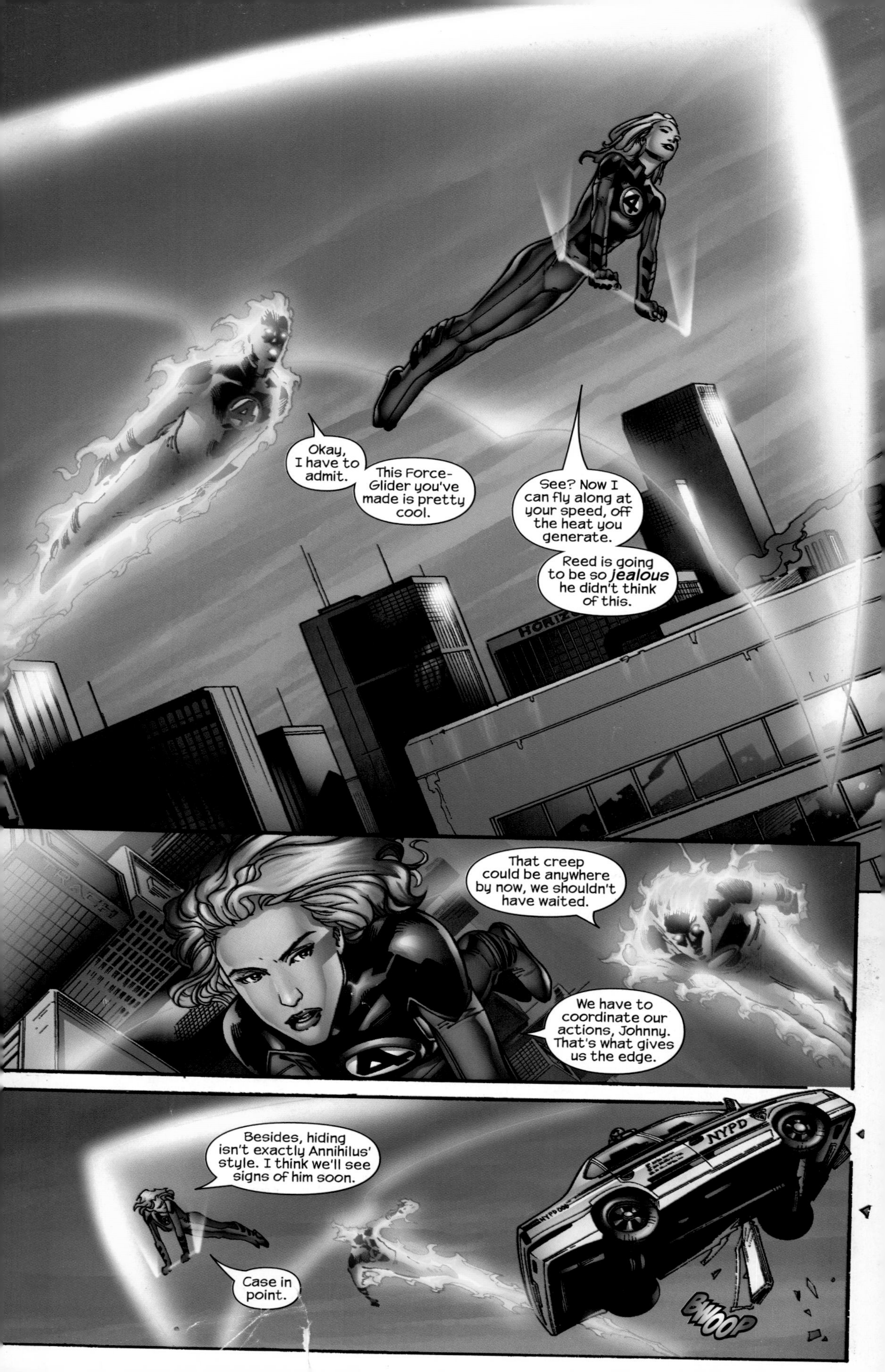

Okay, I have to admit.
This Force-Glider you've made is pretty cool.
See? Now I can fly along at your speed, off the heat you generate.
Reed is going to be so *jealous* he didn't think of this.
That creep could be anywhere by now, we shouldn't have waited.
We have to coordinate our actions, Johnny. That's what gives us the edge.
Besides, hiding isn't exactly Annihilus' style. I think we'll see signs of him soon.
Case in point.
NYPD
BWOOP

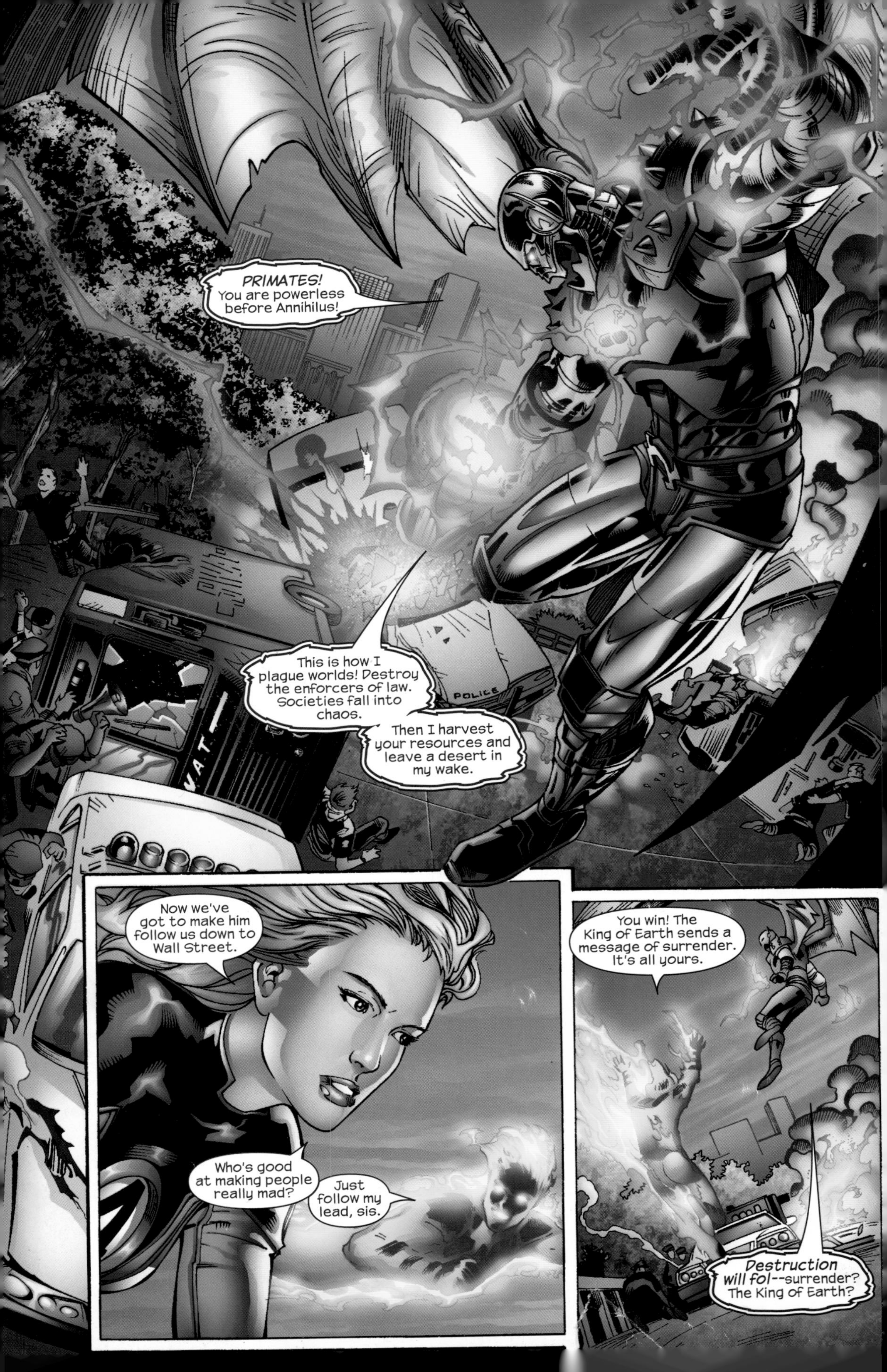
PRIMATES! You are powerless before Annihilus!
This is how I plague worlds! Destroy the enforcers of law. Societies fall into chaos.
Then I harvest your resources and leave a desert in my wake.
POLICE
Now we've got to make him follow us down to Wall Street.
Who's good at making people really mad?
Just follow my lead, sis.
You win! The King of Earth sends a message of surrender. It's all yours.
Destruction will fol--surrender? The King of Earth?

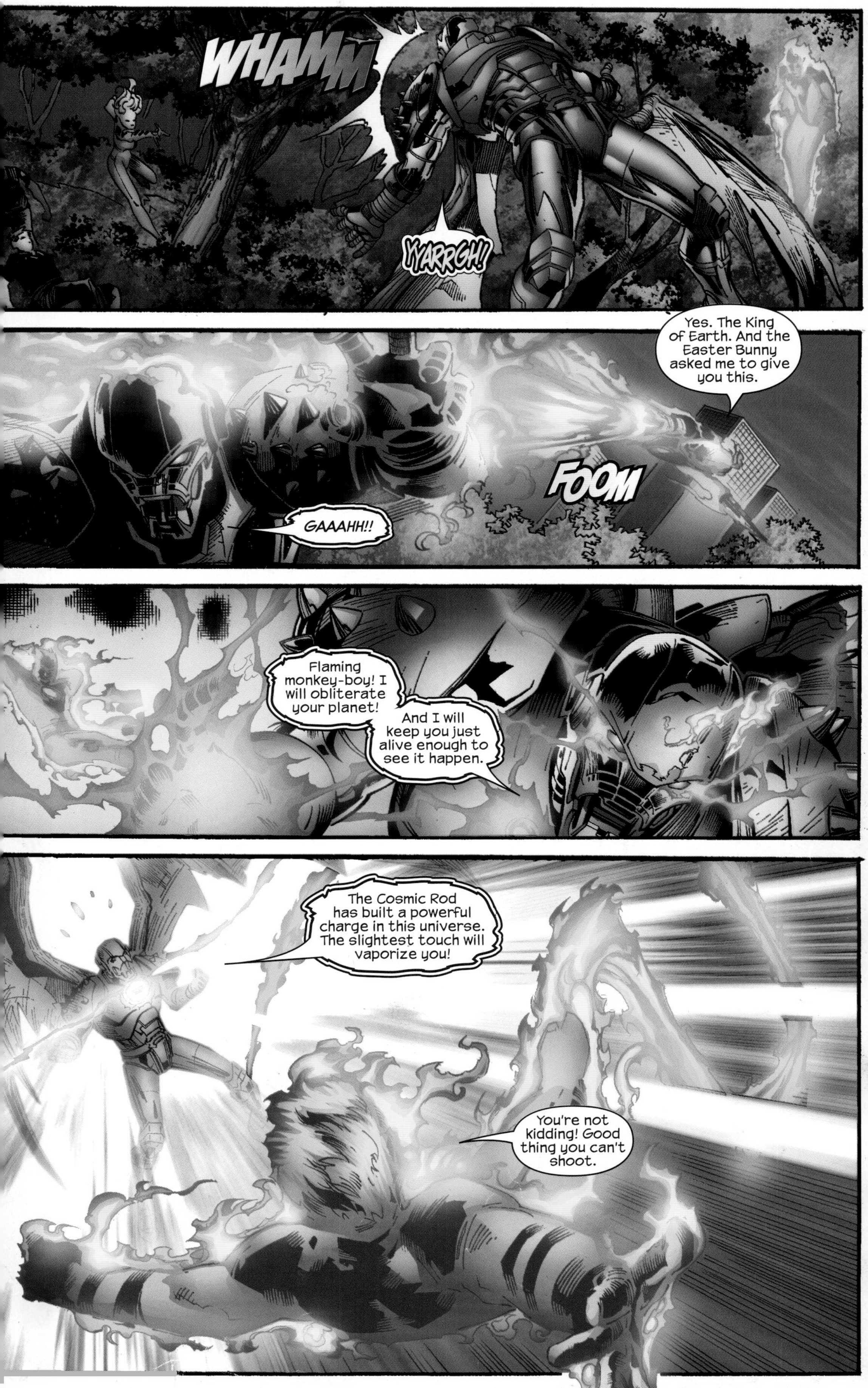
WHAMM
YYARRGH!
Yes. The King of Earth. And the Easter Bunny asked me to give you this.
FOOM
GAAAHH!!
Flaming monkey-boy! I will obliterate your planet!
And I will keep you just alive enough to see it happen.
The Cosmic Rod has built a powerful charge in this universe. The slightest touch will vaporize you!
You're not kidding! Good thing you can't shoot.

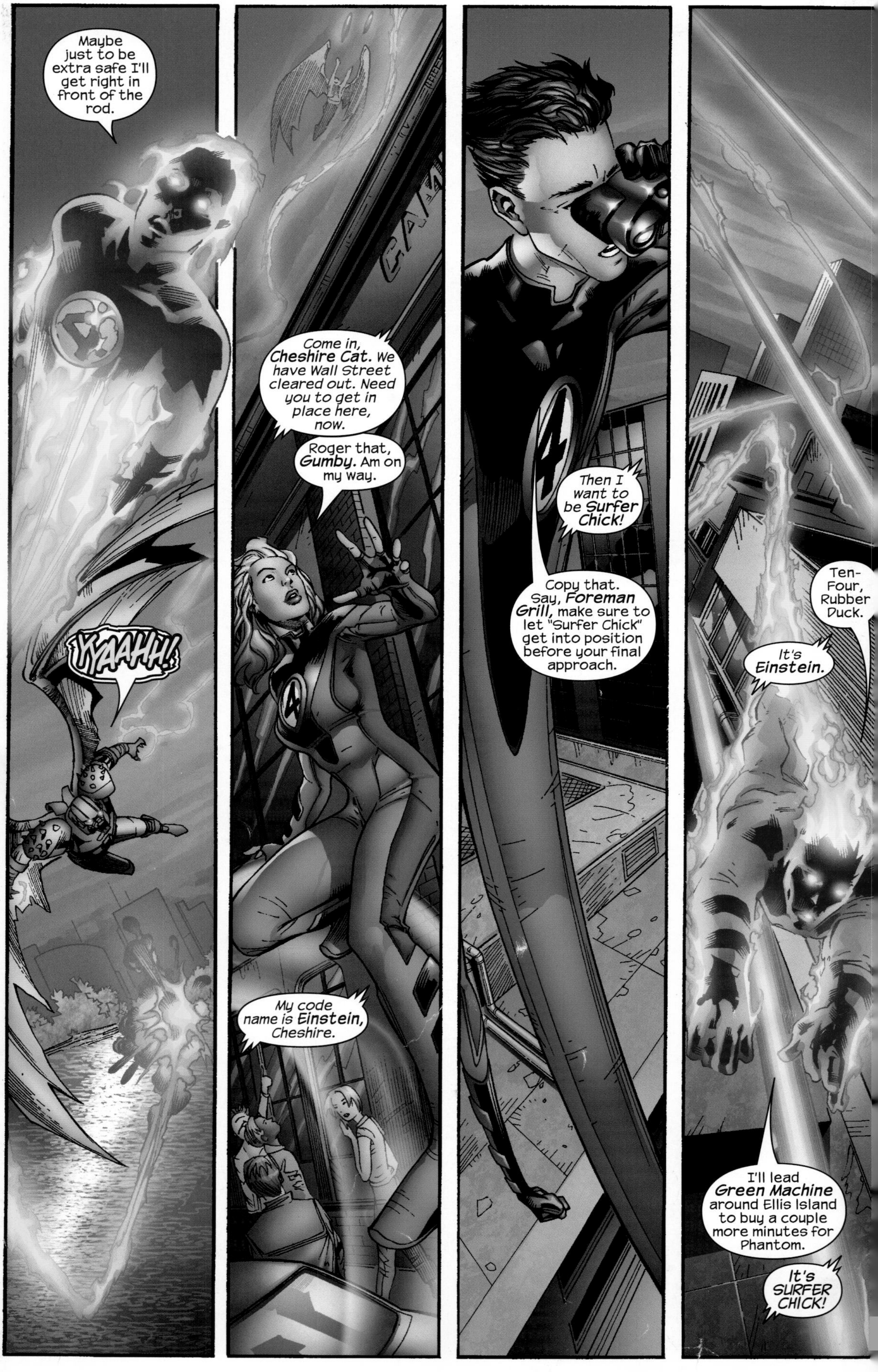

Maybe just to be extra safe I'll get right in front of the rod.
YAAHH!
Come in, **Cheshire Cat.** We have Wall Street cleared out. Need you to get in place here, now.
Roger that, **Gumby.** Am on my way.
My code name is **Einstein,** Cheshire.
Then I want to be **Surfer Chick!**
Copy that. Say, **Foreman Grill,** make sure to let "Surfer Chick" get into position before your final approach.
Ten-Four, Rubber Duck.
It's **Einstein.**
I'll lead **Green Machine** around Ellis Island to buy a couple more minutes for Phantom.
It's SURFER CHICK!

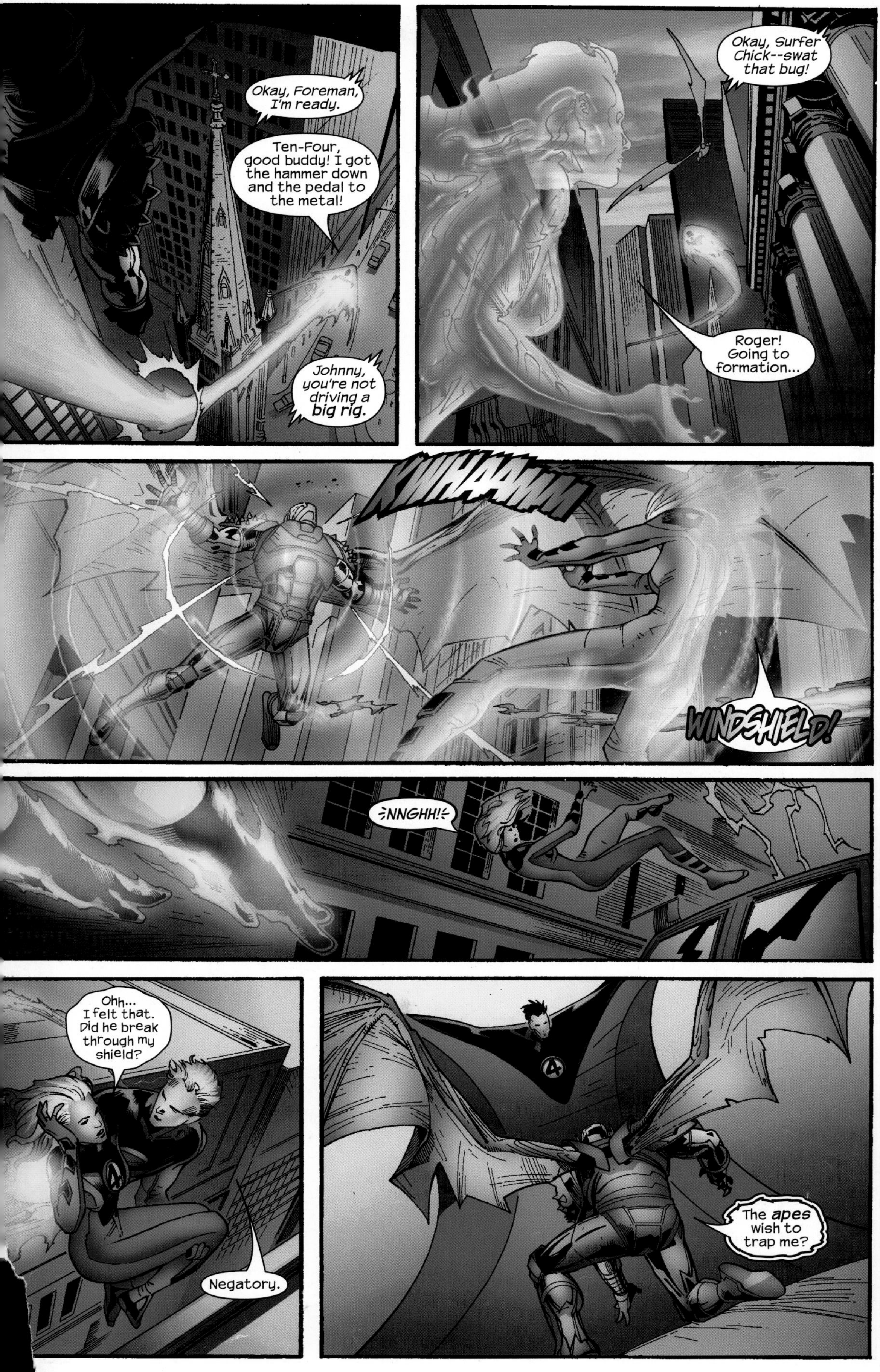
Okay, Foreman, I'm ready.
Ten-Four, good buddy! I got the hammer down and the pedal to the metal!
Johnny, you're not driving a big rig.
Okay, Surfer Chick--swat that bug!
Roger! Going to formation...
KWHAMM
WINDSHIELD!
NNGHH!
Ohh... I felt that. Did he break through my shield?
Negatory.
The apes wish to trap me?

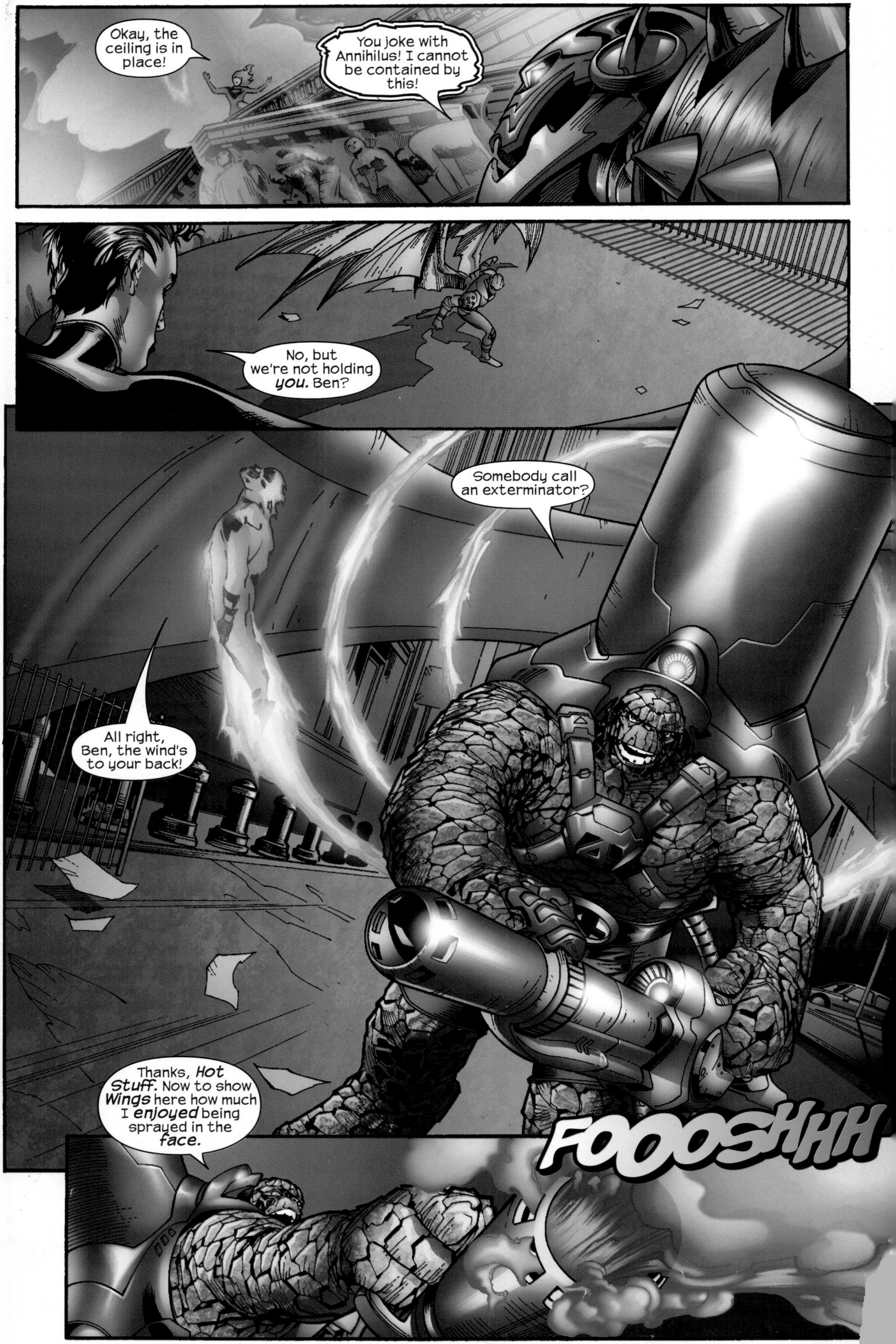
Okay, the ceiling is in place!
You joke with Annihilus! I cannot be contained by this!
No, but we're not holding *you.* Ben?
Somebody call an exterminator?
All right, Ben, the wind's to your back!
Thanks, *Hot Stuff.* Now to show *Wings* here how much I *enjoyed* being sprayed in the *face.*
FOOOSHHH

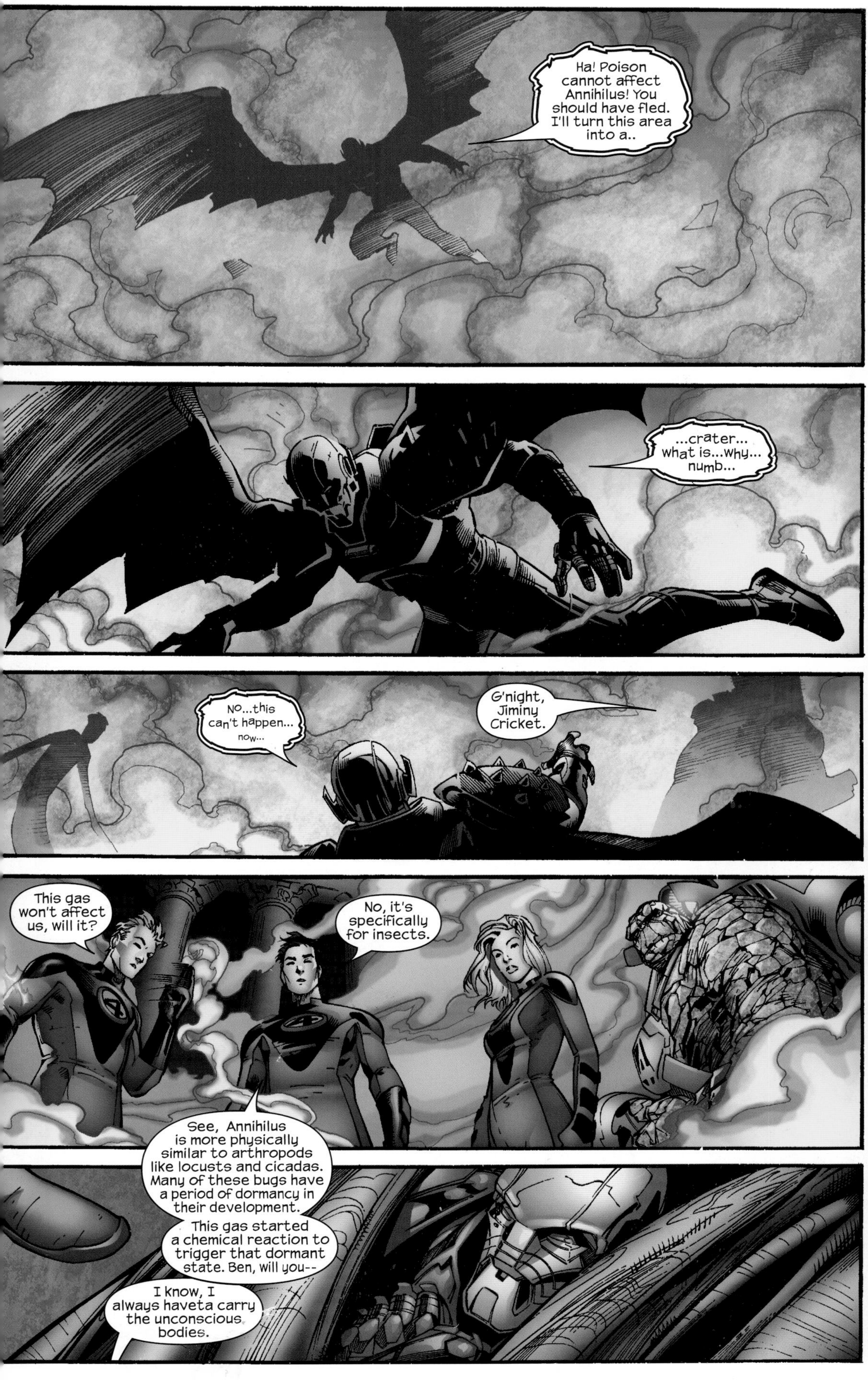
Ha! Poison cannot affect Annihilus! You should have fled. I'll turn this area into a..
...crater... what is...why... numb...
No...this can't happen... now...
G'night, Jiminy Cricket.
This gas won't affect us, will it?
No, it's specifically for insects.
See, Annihilus is more physically similar to arthropods like locusts and cicadas. Many of these bugs have a period of dormancy in their development.
This gas started a chemical reaction to trigger that dormant state. Ben, will you--
I know, I always haveta carry the unconscious bodies.

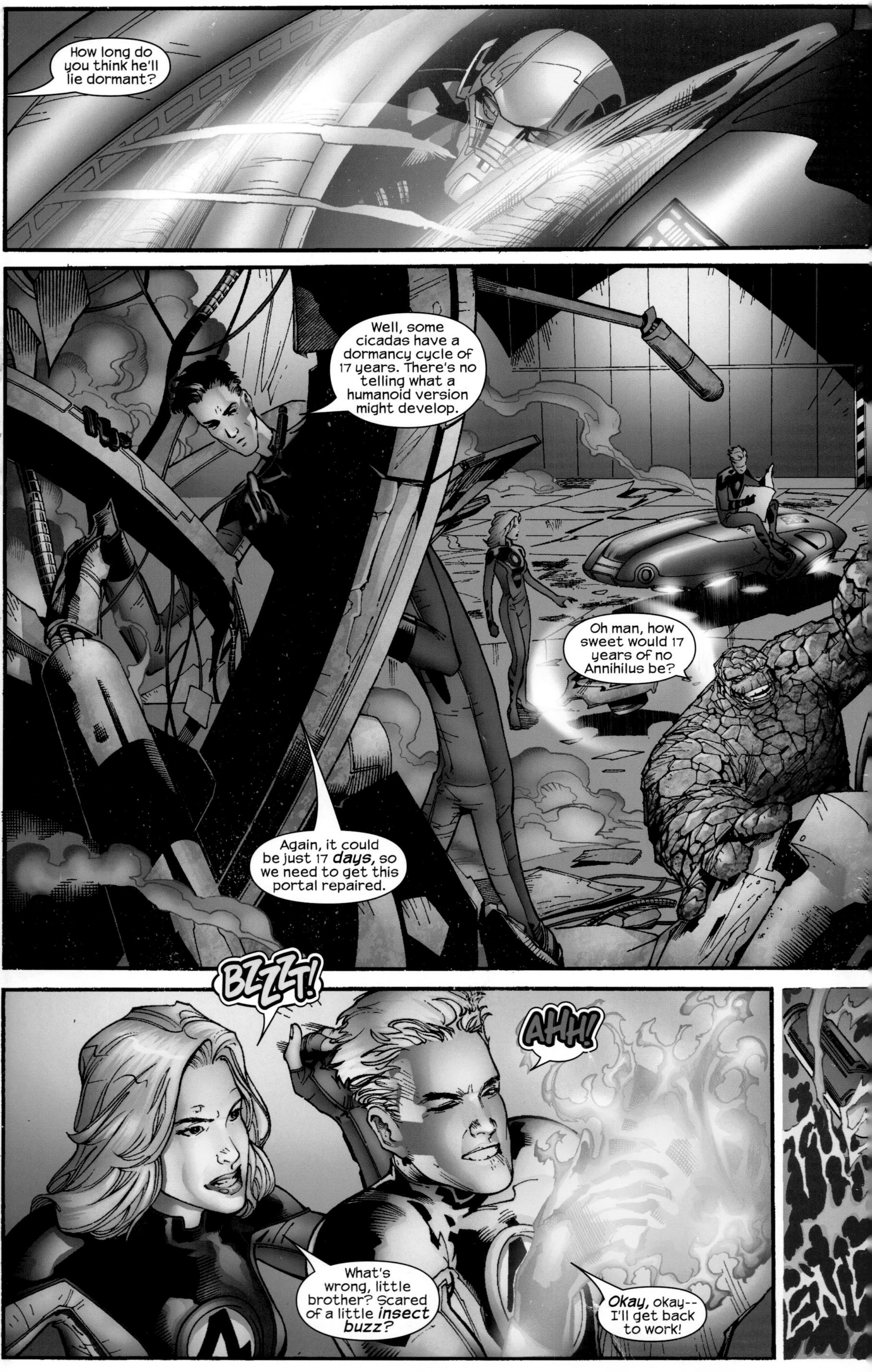
How long do you think he'll lie dormant?
Well, some cicadas have a dormancy cycle of 17 years. There's no telling what a humanoid version might develop.
Oh man, how sweet would 17 years of no Annihilus be?
Again, it could be just 17 *days,* so we need to get this portal repaired.
BZZZT!
AHH!
What's wrong, little brother? Scared of a little *insect buzz?*
Okay, okay-- I'll get back to work!